BLUE RIDGE SHADOWS

OMA BOYD

Enjoy the journey !

Oma Boyd

Orchard Hill Press

Contact the Author: omaboyd@yahoo.com

FOR ERIN AND JOSH

CONTENTS

"But shun profane and vain babblings: for they will increase unto more ungodliness…" II Timothy 2:16

Descending Orchard Gap Mountain Road the views are breathtaking of the valley and mountains beyond. Coves safely tucked in the shadows hold forgotten secrets firmly to their breasts. Pilot Mountain with its spiny back hunched safely in Piedmont North Carolina stands several miles to the south.

I grieve for the misunderstandings many mountain people endured. Some such as my Dandelion were labeled with cruel unforgiving descriptions, which they lived with daily and carried to their graves. Dandelion was labeled a bastard, an orphan and a retard with a special "gift" or as some called it witchery in that era of misunderstandings.

THE FOUNDLING

Dandelion grabbed the familiar vine and hoisted her skinny young body up the side of Buzzard Rock. She sat down on the spiny peak and drew her knees underneath her chin, hugging her calico dress tight to her ankles. Watching silver smoke swirling upward in a straight stream from Uncle Ennis' stone chimney at the base of Squirrel's Spur, she smelled the moistness on the air. Clumps of laurels at the foot of the hill marked his place. Sweet cold water gushed forth, even in summer droughts. People out walking knew his as an abundant spring they could count on always flowing. Uncle Ennis chipped chestnut shingles with a froe and built a lean-to against a tall granite rock. When he emptied a milk crock he washed it right there and turned it up on a makeshift shelf to dry. Overflow swirled over mossy rocks and meandered in a snake like trail down to join the head waters of Ed's falls, the largest waterfall in the mountain. Early morning fog burned away leaving a clear view of the spray coming from the cascading water.

Dandelion thought of the Indians from Wilmington Mama Ellen told about camping at the base of the falls. She felt the smoothness of the big, rounded out rock she waded in on hot days. Mama Ellen said the Indians made it to wash their fresh killed meat and vegetables in when they summered up here to hunt.

Out the ridge is their burying ground. A group of five men came up here years ago hunting for that graveyard. They wanted permission to dig. Mama Ellen didn't tell them she didn't own the land that far over. Staring dead cold in their eyes she pointed to the way back down the mountain. She said, "I reckon it is best to let their bones rest. Some things are sacred, and I reckon that ought to be one of 'em."

Straight ahead fifty miles to the east, Pilot Knob juts skyward with its stiff, spiked spine hunched against the winds that sweep over and around Buzzard Rock.

If anything is sacred to Dandelion it is this rock. The mountain completely surrounds the land below making a bowl shape. The winds blow over the people and their ground ain't steep and rocky.

Some of them make out like they live in God's thumb print. "The good Lord may have sure enough wallowed out a hole with his thumb for them to live in," Dandelion says, but she wouldn't trade a rock on this mountainside for all their flat land.

Dandelion thought about how she came to be here. Mama Ellen, with pity in her eyes, told Dandelion about the day her brother, Burl, brought her home. He got her from Black Tate's widow. Mama Ellen told the story over and over, how the widow Tate was up in her orchard picking up windfalls to dry when she heard a little squeaky whine. She thought an old mammy cat had dropped her kittens close by. She crept over to the last row of apple trees where the orchard stopped and the pine trees started and saw a rusty stovepipe partially covered by fallen tree branches. Getting on her knees she slowly tugged on the corner of a dingy rag sticking out of the flue. A newborn baby slid through the opening wrapped in the sooty cloth. Burl was up the hill pulling poison oak out of the Winesap trees so the pickers could start work when he heard Widow Tate screaming. He ran down there not knowing what to expect. She couldn't speak a sensible word. Widow Tate pointed to the bundle still lying on the ground and took off in a lope mumbling and waving her arms.

Burl crept closer to the spot where she pointed, waiting for movement in the leaves or a rattler to strike. His squinted eyes were carefully inspecting the ground when they settled on a small puckered face.

He did the only thing he knew to do and that was to take the infant to Ellen.

Ellen heard Burl shouting when he crossed the footbridge. She dropped the wet overalls into the soak tub and rushed around the pear tree to catch a glimpse of him waving something in his hands. Was it rags? Why was he shouting like a drunken fool?

She never knew what to expect. One minute he was humble and the next his wild haired temper would back up the toughest man. She reasoned that was why people around the mountain called him, Judge Stump-Weed. The Judge part he earned honestly from the family, because he was constantly confronting people and butting into their business. Stump-weed was added on by the locals, because he never filled out and made no size at all.

"What is it?"

"Come see for yourself," he stuck the bundle out in her direction jumping the woodpile to meet her on the other side.

"Lord Jesus!" her breath escaped like a sigh.

"What have you done?" she whispered realizing it was a newborn infant.

The weight holding him seemed to lift as soon as Ellen took the baby and wrapped it tightly in her apron. His legs collapsed forcing him back on his rump in the splintered chips. Closing his eyes and relaxing in the knowledge that he was free of that thing in those filthy rags eased the tension.

He had helped birth enough calves to know how messy they were but generally a brute's mother cared enough about her offspring to lick the blood off while it was still damp. Never had he seen one caked and dried and reeking like this tiny thing.

Remembering it was still alive, brought Burl to his feet. He saw Ellen standing at the four-poster bed with a square of clean sheet over the quilted coverlet, and the little knotted bundle in a fold on one end. The small room reeked of fumes from the strong homemade camphor she was dribbling on a scorched rag covering the crusted navel cord. She took a small cloth square filled it with white sugar rolled it up in a cone shape and greased the tip-end with cow's butter so it would be moist enough to entice the infant to open her mouth.

It was days before Dandelion was strong enough to latch onto anything so they fed her from a glass dropper. When she pursed her lips and received the liquid drops, Ellen encouraged her to take more by telling her what a dandy of a girl she was. It was late one night when Burl woke up and named her. It was written to him that she was Dandelion, no middle name, Johnston.

Mama Ellen loved to tell how ugly and deformed she looked and how she reckoned she'd grow out of it . . . someday.

"If dandelions were hard to grow, they would be most welcome on any lawn."

~Andrew Mason

ROCK

"If'n I had wings I would leap straight up and out, catch me an upstream draft and float out over them clouds," Dandelion said from her rock perch.

Sunlight bounced off a rusty piece of tin flopping on Tycie's barn roof. Her barn set a short distance in the cove below Buzzard Rock.

Dandelion remembered the time Tycie's biggest boy, Mullin, found her female ailment pills she had hidden in the barn and emptied a whole bottle in the cats trough of warm cow's milk, killing just about every cat in walking distance of their place.

Tycie was mean to Mullin and his younger sister, Lissie, because they weren't really hers. The Dutchman had them by Millie Law.

When she died he went searching for the young'uns a new mother and married Tycie. Some people scolded him for courting and marrying so quickly after his wife's burial. The Dutchman explained it by saying, "Huh, I reckon Millie Law is just as dead now as she will ever be!"

Other people round the mountain said Tycie's daddy gave him a two-toned Jersey cow to take Tycie off his hands. Mama Ellen said, "The Dutchman didn't have a choice. The stupid thing couldn't raise a garden without help!"

Tycie and the old Dutchman had five young'uns of their own within six years of marrying. Mullin and his sister were forgotten. They were left to their own devices, roaming through the mountain and doing without.

Mama Ellen called them strays. She put fried meat and hunks of wheat bread in a handled bucket and tied it in an oak tree next to the spring. She put it up high, knotting the wire bail handle with a stout string, so the critters couldn't get it. Mullin and Lissie slipped up there and ate. Sometimes Dandelion hid under a laurel and watched them, but never mentioned it to anyone. It made her feel close to them to share their secret.

When the sick feeling of longing for the unknown settled on her hard, she thought of them as her real family. The three bound with an invisible string of despair.

She found no comfort in Mama Ellen's words, "Dandelion, just because you look and act different don't mean you ain't right in the head. Why, you can cook and tote a water bucket good as anybody."

Dandelion let out a shrill war whoop, relieving the tightness in her throat, woo, whoop…echoed around the mountain.

THE FEVER

"It's weathered all night." Ellen said checking the rag chinking in the cracks of the window frame.

"We need some light and air in this room. I do believe I will smother to death in this heat." Ellen pulled back the lacy fabric from the window.

Green waxy leaves draped the outside of the glass panes like a shroud making it impossible to see beyond the boxwood; cowering in wait for the wind to heft its massive body against the house.

Pap planted the boxwood going on seventy years ago. He dug the hole for it too close to the house. Mam told him it would grow in on the window and she wouldn't be able to see out but he didn't listen. Mam, as sweet and kind-hearted as she was, despised his hateful stubbornness and the evergreen with its spiny, dead limbs snatching and pawing the glass panes. On the morning of his death Mam went to the window, pulled up the shade and told him to look out if he thought he could see anything.

Although Ellen didn't like the boisterous shrub, she had never felt the grip of hatred for the boxwood as strongly as today. Dumping the fever warmed water into the ash hopper and adding a dipper of fresh; she carefully soaked the cloth and squeezed it out before placing it back on Dandelion's forehead. The child's faint pulse was barely a tick beneath her fingertips. Taking the wall calendar down and circling the days she counted backwards the dates with the circles. One, two, three... this was the third day Dandelion had laid, barely moving, with her knees drawn in to her chest like a new born baby. Her tongue coated and mouth so sore she had refused even a taste of water during the night. Mama Ellen eased Dandelion's sweaty gown over her head. "Got to dry this wet sheet too," she said. "The young'un will take pneumonia fever if the air chills her. A fiery tinge of red covered a rough round spot underneath Dandelion's arm. She then looked closer; there was a blotch of chafed skin as big as her hand on the inside of her thigh.

Mama Ellen whispered the same prayer she had said over Dandy for three days. It seemed to bring her little comfort. She sternly reminded herself what Dr. Gates had said when he checked her at the first of the week. He was thinking it was scarlet fever. There were two other cases over in The Hollow. He posted a sign on their front door when he left and told Ellen it was very contagious for the first few days and for them not to let anyone in the house. He had assured Ellen that Dandelion's fever would break when she sweated out the rash. Ellen's thoughts were interrupted by Mullin's voice coming from the yard.

"Burl, crack the door a slit and see what Mullin needs. He is out there under the apple tree hollering his fool head off." Burl pulled back the latch and stepped around the sign, its bold red lettering warned, Quarantined.

"Hey, that you, Mullin?"

"Yep, Lissie sent me to see if the fever has broke."

"Not yet. Ellen has every quilt in the house packed on that young'un and I have kept the fire roaring all night. She hasn't had a bite to eat in three days. A little bit of weak cold coffee until last night and then her tongue was so tender she let it run out the corners of her mouth. Ellen says the inside of her mouth is white with blisters."

"The hell you say! What you going to do?" Mullin's strong words didn't fit his young body and it was more than Burl could take with all the worry on him.

"We doing the best we can! You get on your way."

"Lissie sent Dandelion a present. I reckon I can lay it here for her."

"Get! I will take it in the house."

Burl picked up the bag and took it inside. "Lissie sent something for Dandy."

"What is it? Why it is so flat I don't believe there is nothing in it. It would be just like that fool Tycie to fill a bag of air and send it up here. Heartless heifer she is, but if Mullin said Lissie sent it that means she more in likely, don't know a thing about it. I'll lay it here on the table until Dandy is up to opening it. I don't won't to deprive her of that little bit of joy."

"Burl, help me sit her in this chair so I can strip the bed." Ellen got a warm quilt from the drying rack next to the stove and wrapped Dandelion in it. She changed the bedclothes and got her small frame settled against the feather pillows.

"Look at her hands… fingers, palms and all red as a sunburn and feels like sandpaper."

"I pray she makes a turn and makes it quick…she's so scrawny now ain't no telling what will happen!" Ellen tried to ignore the worry in Burls voice.

"Now the fever is broke I'll have her up by nightfall."

"Here, Dandelion, open up," Mama Ellen commanded, "I know it hurts to swallow, but I have got to dose you with this castor oil. It'll work the poison out."

Dandelion clinched her teeth together. She felt Mama Ellen pinching her nose forcing her to open her mouth. As soon as the vile liquid hit her tongue Mama Ellen blew in her face.

Dandelion lay all afternoon with her knees drawn to help relieve her stomach cramps. It was almost dark when they eased enough for her to notice the paper sack on the table. Four pages from a Burpees seed catalog were sewn together along the inner edge with white darning thread. The 1945 cover featured a new red Rhubarb Chard, in its natural shape…a great V. To the left of the V was a new orange-colored Jubilee Tomato; Above the V was a cluster of large, plump carrots. The following pages were filled with purple violets, red roses, yellow tulips and dark blue clusters of grapes posing on the slick paper. They looked so real Dandelion could smell the sweetness from the flowers and her mouth watered remembering how she loved the juice of grapes.

"Oh, look." Dandelion turned the picture of the roses towards Mama Ellen.

"Do you reckon you could take this thread out without breaking it? I want you to take the pages apart and stick them on the wall where I can see them every minute I am awake." Mama Ellen noticed how Dandelion's arms trembled from the slight effort of holding the pages a short while. At least with her fever gone she stood a good chance of getting stronger.

"Let us dance in the sun, wearing wild flowers in our hair..."

~Susan Polis Shutz

CONVERSION

Burl leaned in a straight back chair against the backside of the house waiting for daybreak. He lit a cigarette, opening and shutting his mouth like a guppy fish out of water; smoke rings rose toward the dark sky. He cursed Ellen's rooster, calling him a peaked face son of a bitch for crowing while the air was still black.

"If you had a brain one in that dottling head you'd stay at roost til it's time for Ellen to get up!" he said kicking his legs in rhythm to his sing song voice. "Lord knows, it's little enough peace I see around here and with all that cock-a-doodling you'll have Ellen up and she'll be at me to fetch this or tote the other."

The beginnings of sunshine spreading horizontally over the hill lighted the springhouse path. "I may as well get the water bucket and go fill it before Ellen starts in on me." He fumed, crossing the kitchen doorjamb and grabbing up the empty pail. Cautiously picking his way along the dew covered grass and rounding the first bend sure to hide him from view of his house, he bent over and shuffled beneath the long, green weeping branches of the willow tree. Kneeling close to the mossy trunk he tried to pray: "Lord, Lord…help me."

He had been up all night studying on religion. Dandy's sickness did it to him. Burl convinced himself she was depending on him to make her well and it scared him to think if she died he would be responsible. The air in the room seemed especially warm to Burl all night. He perspired profusely. Usually he was dense when he tried to remember things, but it seemed he memorized every word of scripture he had heard Ellen speak and every verse of the hymns she sang to Dandelion. It was like a recording playing over and over in his head or a heavy ebony shadow that wouldn't fade.

Chunking the wood fire in the night, his legs gave way and he had to hold to the metal bed rail to keep from sinking down onto the rough plank floor. When he regained enough strength to walk, he went outside searching for something to hold him and heal Dandy.

Burl kicked a pile of leaves at the base of a rotting tree next to the springhouse and uncovered a half-gallon of corn likker. He checked on it every morning to make sure it was still there. The metal ring was rusting away from the Ball lid that sealed it. The devils brew, he thought, that's what Preacher Cable called it.

He stepped up on the foot log, casting his eyes over the spring with the little lizards darting around the cistern. Burl peered out the path and satisfied he was alone he took on the preacher's tone and faithfully tried to pray aloud but again words failed him.

His hands tingled. He shook them from one side of his body to the other. His legs trembled and jerked. He couldn't stand still. Staggering in a hopping motion, he looked around thinking perhaps he had stepped on a yellow jackets nest. A four-foot wide streak of light poured though the overgrowth onto the waxy leaves of the laurel bushes.

"What in the . . ." his speech was slurred and he couldn't remember anything but the jar of moonshine he still held in his hands. The beaded brew cast a golden glow. He carefully placed it back in its resting place and arranged the dried leaves over it so if anybody walked by they couldn't tell the place had been disturbed. He held the tin drinking can under the cold spring water, it sloshed out wetting his shirt sleeves, with trembling hands he filled Ellen's bucket. He knew she would be up and waiting.

He quietly entered through the kitchen door and placed the water bucket on the homemade oak table. His chair was still outside and his Bible laid at his place setting, undisturbed. Opened to the book of Job where he had left it. Preacher Cable had convinced him that if he asked sincerely the Lord would reveal the words of the scriptures to him, although he had never learned to read. He picked the Bible up and took it outside sitting in his chair he glared at the typed words on the thin page. "Ask, and you shall find," he said bowing his head after making sure Ellen was occupied inside the house. The warm sunshine soothed him and soon he nodded his hands relaxed and the Bible slipped quietly to the ground.

He saw the Heavens open and Jesus stood in the sky holding his hands out for Burl to touch. He saw the nail scars on Jesus' palms, his brown hair blew around his shoulders, and his flowing snowy gown hid his sandal clad feet. Ellen and Dandelion stepped forward from a white cloud with their arms intertwined.

Burl heard Jesus faintly calling his name as they all disappeared from view leaving him standing alone. He opened his eyes and saw Ellen.

"Did you see him?" Burl questioned.

"What is the matter with you?" she asked picking the Bible up and dusting it off.

Burl walked the short path to the spring and uncovered the half gallon jar. The fragile can ring fell off when he touched it. A rusty sharp prong pricked his finger. He pulled it out and pinched the cut between his forefinger and thumb squeezing hard trying to get it to bleed. He watched one single droplet of blood fall as if by slow motion and land on the top of his boot. The rubber seal of the lid was so loose he flicked it off with his fingernail and slowly tipped the jug until he got a taste on his tongue. The stout, aged whiskey burned his throat cutting loose the choking feeling that pestered him.

"Forgive me," he said taking a drink. By the time he got back to the house he had drank just enough to calm his nerves and help him sleep. He slept deep and long, waking just before sunset

He needed to talk with someone other than Ellen. The Lord knew he could never discuss his inner most thoughts with her. Preacher Cable might have some answers but he was on top the mountain holding services and wouldn't be back for at least a week.

Ellen interrupted his thoughts to tell him his supper was on the table.

"Come eat, Dandy took a couple spoons of clear, tater broth."

Burl balked at the very idea of food. Stepping outside, as the purplish hue of the setting sun cast its last faint color in the west, he disappeared down the springhouse path.

"Can we conceive what humanity would be if it did not know the flowers?"

~Maurice Maeterlinck

BASTARD CHILD

Mama Ellen selfishly instilled a fear of the unknown in Dandelion. She didn't go to school because it was thought she was too slow minded to learn. Neither was she allowed to leave the property line, which was fenced. The stacked rocks towered like the walls of a prison keeping Dandelion inside.

Mama Ellen cautioned her repeatedly about eating poisonous plants. Dandelion found out, at an early age, about the orange colored persimmon growing by their spring. The fruit drew her mouth inside out in a stiff pucker if she tried to eat one before the first hard freeze of late fall. Then they were soft and mushy. She didn't like the taste or the feel of the goo on her tongue.

It was here, at the mountain spring, she found Mullin and Lissie waiting for her. They had crawled through a large gaping hole to surprise Dandelion. Mullin immediately showed her the oak tree hanging heavy with fresh green balls. He burst one open and ate the tender casing.

"Scaredy cat, scaredy cat," Mullin taunted her until she ate one and Dandelion waited in terror, to die from the poison, until bedtime. But when Mullin introduced her to the sweet taste of wild honey locust blooms she loved them. It was the second week in June and the gullies and creeks were overflowing from the hearty spring rains. The way Mullin showed her to put the white blossoms, dangling from thorny stems, into her mouth and suck out their nectar was pure joy. He picked the first bunch of flowers and offered her the next. She pricked her fingers on thorns until Mullin showed her to reach in from the top of the limb and sneak in on the tips where the tender clusters hung.

It was a honey locust tree where Mullin drew, with a stolen pocket knife, the heart shape in the bark and put a straight mark in the middle of it telling Dandelion the line was an "L" which stood for the word love. He drew an arrow catty-corner to the middle of the heart and said that meant he had shot it for his intended.

Dandelion wanted to ask him if he was in love but when she made eye contact with him he snorted and scuffed the ground with his feet. Then he angrily cut the bark gouging out a shape that reminded her of a hen's egg and carved a deep slit in the center. He looked at her then, a quick glance, directly in the eyes and said, "There!"

Dandelion had never thought of Mullin as being in love but now she wondered if he meant she was his intended. Her face flushed but she wasn't sure why and for the first time she saw Mullin as opposite of her. There was something different about the way he looked and smelled. His wet odor reminded her of stump water. It scared and thrilled her at the same time.

"This is my tree now," he said. "I have put my mark on it and it will only grow larger with the passing of time."

Dandelion wasn't sure what he was talking about. It was all confusing, the way she felt weak and dizzy intensified his stench and made her stomach queasy.

"Want to go to the falls?" he asked walking ahead. She followed close behind with her head bent and her eyes cast down. Every time he ran off she tried to catch up but it was hard with her head swimming and the ground floating at her feet. She had never been out in the trees alone and the afternoon light played tricks with the shadows casting dark places in a way that frightened her.

Today was the first time Dandelion had crossed the boundary fence. Mama Ellen had reminded her not to wander out of sight of the house, and if she heard her beating the bottom of the wash tub to come running. But, today was special. It was Dandelion's birthday. At least Mama Ellen said it was close enough to count as the day she was born. It was June the eleventh when Burl found her and Mama Ellen said that if she was born one minute before midnight her birthday would be the tenth but she couldn't see how Dandelion could have survived all night stuffed in a stove pipe so June 11, was what she wrote in the Bible.

Mullin jumped the creek; Dandelion mimicked his actions and landed in the wet bog. When she pulled her feet out, her shoes came off covered in black muck. She walked the rest of the way uphill carrying her shoes in her hands. Mullin climbed the steep incline and got on the mountain road. Just before they were to re-enter the trees to the falls they passed Aunt Leodia's house. Her door was propped open. Mullin said they should stop in and see if she had some biscuits left over from dinner. He hollered out when they entered the house but no one was home. Mullin went to the cook stove and got a biscuit out of the warmer but Dandelion said she didn't want any.

Mullin walked up behind her and thumped her on the head, "What's that?" he asked. Dandelion turned a page with more writing on it. "That's names of people and dates like is on the calendar." he said, "Pages and pages of names and dates." Dandelion didn't say anything but she felt closed in and hurried for the door and the sunshine in the yard. Mullin followed.

"What's the matter? You sick or something?" he noticed Dandelion's ashen face. And then without her saying a word he knew.

"I bet that is names of the babies Aunt Leodia has delivered wrote in that book."

"Let's go back and look for your name!"

Dandelion felt like he had punched her. She couldn't move. Did he know her real mother's name? She wondered.

Mullin dodged through the door and came back outside holding the book high so Dandelion couldn't touch it. He set down on the bank, out of reach, and flipped the pages.

"This is mostly men's names. Heads of the households I guess."

"What was your daddy's name?"

"You don't know, do you? Don't have any idea who your own daddy was or real mama either."

"Bastard," Mullin rifled the pages looking to see if it went back thirteen years so he could find his own name and date of birth.

"Child alive, look who is here." Aunt Leodia had walked up without being seen and Dandelion spooked. She ran head first into a rambling rose bush, backed out and snagged her dress tail on the chicken wire fence getting it caught so it tore out a chunk as she went. She half staggered and half tumbled down the mountainside where she crawled through the hole in their fence.

She fell down on the ground and lay there. The blue sky was wavy above her. She thought of Mama Ellen and knew she shouldn't have gone off with Mullin. But, she was tired of Mama Ellen's tending. She tended the house, the cows, and the fires in the four rock chimneys. Always making sure the mud-dabbed flue beside of Dandelions bed in the attic was warm before the logs were banked at night.

The next thing she knew she awoke to a metallic ringing in the distance. She saw a man coming towards her from across the field. It was Burl.

"I'll swear and be damned, girl. You gone stone deaf have you?"

"Don't you hear Ellen down yonder beating the bottom out of that confounded tub? Get up and hurry with it. Sometimes you act like you got cow shit for brains!"

Dandelion started to stand but her knees buckled and she fell back in a half sitting and half laying position.

Burl came closer to help her "What in the fiery hell... you look like a she bear has had a hold of you."

He grabbed her right arm to jerk her up. His boxy fingers dug deep into her spindly bones causing him to ease his hold and swing her across his back. She hooked her mud incrusted ankles around his waist, with her arms twined around his thick neck. Dandelion didn't realize how she looked with her thin, kinky hair tied in knots, her dress torn from the waist band in the back and bloody scratches going the whole length of her left arm.

"You may still be a small tike but you are double digit now. About too old for piggy backing, don't you reckon?" Burl's voice had softened.

"Ellen is worried sick about you. She'll want to know what you been up to and from the looks of things I don't reckon she needs to know. Been off exploring have you? I passed that crazy Mullin when I come across the hill. Fool boy jumped behind a pine, thought I couldn't see him!"

Dandelion didn't hear the rest of what Burl said. She didn't care what he thought about Mullin or anything else. She dug her fingers into his Adam's apple hoping she could cut off his airway so he would know how it felt not to be able to get his breath.

"I don't know what has had a hold of you, but you best not let Ellen see you like this. Slip through the side door and clean up. I'll let her know you're all right."

Every year Burl and Ellen worked feverishly to get the new potato vines to produce in time to have the first mess for Dandelion's birthday. It made the day special setting it apart from all the others.

She smelled them when she entered the kitchen. Steam swirled from the red-cobblers as Mama Ellen mashed butter in them and handed the plate to Dandelion. She looked at Dandy's pale shriveled hand and saw it in a way she hadn't noticed before. She was ten in man's years, but Mama Ellen had her doubts she would ever be ten in size and smarts. Leaving the dirty dishes on the table, Ellen took Dandelion into her bedroom and shut the door.

"Dandy, there is something I have been putting off talking to you about," She spoke in a tone she hoped the child could understand. Although Dandelion was at the age of understanding in man's years, Mama Ellen was certain she wouldn't mature to that age even as an adult. She was stunted. A child needs nourishment of the soul as well as its mother's milk to get started right.

"Dandy, I worry about what might happen if I was to not be here anymore. I know what people say about you and the names they call you. Well, child, it ain't right to be cast on in such a way. People in the mountain love to talk. They always have and I reckon they always will. Some use it for entertainment and some plain don't know no better. I don't want you to ever doubt yourself. You are as good as any and better than most."

"There is no doubt who your father is," She watched the child's expressions carefully as she continued, "Dandy, you know the country doctor who travels through these hills and hollows mending the sick and delivering babies?" Mama Ellen thought she recognized a nod even though Dandelion didn't raise her head. "He has been here many times and seen you, child, more than once when you had the fever."

"Dandelion," Mama Ellen couldn't keep the aggravation from her voice. Putting her hand under Dandelion's chin forcing her to make eye contact she said. "Listen to me now, girl. Hold your head up and stand tall...your daddy is an upstanding citizen in this mountain! Your mother cast a spell on the good doctor. She wasn't fit to wipe his shoes but there weren't a thing in the world he could do about it!

She stayed with people through the mountain who was having a new baby. Did the housework, and tended to the other children in the family if there was any."

Mama Ellen described her beauty in a way which colored a vivid picture in Dandelion's mind: Thick silky hair flowing to her hips earned her the nickname Babe by all who knew her. Her dark moist eyes pierced a man's soul at a glance. She was a willowy beauty that ran through this mountain as wild and free as morning glory vine.

No pessimist ever discovered the secret of the stars,
or sailed to an uncharted land,
or opened a new doorway for the human spirit.

~ Helen Keller ~

FUNERAL

Dandelion moved through the broom-straw as effortlessly as the wind, or so it seemed. The breeze danced along the fussy tops covering each track she made in the row. You might have been able to see her bent body from the rock ledge if you were looking down, but to just pass along the road you would have never known she was there.

"Come at dinner," she remembered Lissie saying.

As soon as Mama Ellen set the bean-pot off the table she rushed out and disappeared around the back corner of the kitchen.

The noonday sun bore into the top of Dandelion's head. She wished she had put on her hat. At the far edge of the field she saw the clearing. Squatting down and peeping out she saw the three pronged oak Lissie had told her about. She rushed forward with head bent, and bumped into Lissie making her hit the hard bark on the tree. A large group of people were gathering around the church door some going inside and others mingling around talking.

"Is it here yet?"

"Not yet, but any minute I reckon."

Dandelion wanted so badly to see it. "How do you know Lissie?"

"Well, they will have to take her inside the church. I figure all we need to do...hush, look here it comes! Do you see it?"

Everyone had gone inside the church except the men standing at the door. Slowly the black hearse pulled in and stopped. A man dressed in a suit got out and opened the back doors. The men walked around and pulled out a long, steel casket. This was the first hearse Dandelion had ever seen. Also it was the first funeral in a church.

"I can't see," Dandelion complained, "how we going to see her in that box with it sealed?"

"We ain't, we going to peep in the window when they open her for viewing."

"How you know they will open it?"

"They always open them. I have been to just about every funeral they have had out here this year."

"But this one's different Lissie. You know it is." Dandelion had heard Mama Ellen telling Burl how they had burnt the mattress the woman died on even her quilts. Took it all outside and burned it so nobody else would take the TB.

"Yes it's different all right but they will still have it the same way as the rest I reckon. They will open the lid and the family will walk by and look in the box first. Then all these people that have come early will go up there and that is when we will look in the window. The room is so crowded they will be watching each other instead of us."

The large windows were propped open with sticks so the breeze could help cool the room. Another black vehicle came up the drive and parked. It was stuffed full of flowers. The man entered the church and came out with four little girls dressed in their Sunday best. Dandelion loved their shiny patent leather shoes and lacy topped socks folded neatly at their skinny ankles. They carried the wreaths of blooms to the front of the church and a man set them around the altar. The girls kept coming in and going out until the front was full and he placed flowers, on tall stands, against the wall behind the pulpit.

"Law, it's pitiful to think of the preacher with them little young'uns and no wife." Lissie said.

Dandelion couldn't see how it made any difference between the preacher's wife and Lissie's own mother who died. To Lissie and

Mama Ellen you would have thought one of God's angels herself had left this earthly home and gone to the pearly gates. In Dandelion's mind she was just a woman same as Millie Law had been. No better cause she married a preacher.

The crowd was seated and the flowers placed when they rolled the casket in front of the pulpit. The man in black opened the lid and placed a spray of red and white carnations which reached from her waist to her feet and then hung off the end of the blue steel box. He then put white netting over the woman's face, and stepped aside.

Dandelion saw one brown curl before the netting blocked her view. The women were sniffling and wiping tears with bleached handkerchiefs. Dandelion hung her head and wiped at her eyes. The mournful music floated through the opened windows, "Come home, come home, it's supper time..."

The preacher and his two girls went to the front just like Lissie had said they would do. He held his youngest daughter up so she could touch her Mommy's hands. Instead she grabbed her pearl necklace and while he worked to free the child's grasp the larger girl bent and kissed her cold face.

They sat on the front pew, and the congregation arose and walked up the narrow aisle in pairs. Dandelion and Lissie couldn't see anything, but the women and men filing by the window.

"Come on," Lissie stepped around the church corner.

"Wait!" Dandelion begged. But Lissie had already got to the door and was going inside. Dandelion hung her head down and looked at the dirty plank floor until she was stopped by the casket. The air was musky with the scent of Rose of Paris perfume and dead flowers. A big busted woman pressed against Dandelion and moved her along out of view of the box. Dandelion didn't look up to see if she knew the woman. She felt if she didn't look at the crowd they wouldn't see her. Mama Ellen would have a fit if she knew Dandelion went inside the church in her wrinkled dingy dress and no shoes. It was Lissie's fault she was here with this sick smell stuck in the back of her throat. Old Tycie didn't care where Lissie went or what she looked like.

Dandelion and Lissie had just got back outside to look in the window when Lissie said, "God Almighty!"

Dandelion looked just in time to see Maude Little collapse in a heap on the floor. Her dotted dress was up over her fat legs. Her stocking garters cutting into the hanging flesh below her knees.

"I reckon with all that powder and paint on her face; it has cut her air off." Lissie sneered.

The preacher came forth swishing a cardboard fan with a picture of Jesus on it. They hovered around Maude until Dandelion couldn't see her legs, or anything else.

"The Lord is my Shepherd," Dandelion wiped her eyes.

"Hush up your mumbling." The choir kept singing. A woman in the back row shouted sending shivers through the room.

"Look," Lissie pushed Dandelion in front of the opened window, "Maude has wiggled her dress up over her big rump."

Someone held a small bottle under Maude's nose. In just a minute she raised a hand waving it away.

"What's that?" Lissie questioned.

"Camphor."

"Ain't no such a thing! Who ever saw camphor in that small a bottle?"

Three preachers took turns at the pulpit before they closed the service. Dandelion watched as the deacons of the church lined up by the casket and carried it down the aisle. She and Lissie hid behind a monument and peeped around it as the crowd made their way to the gravesite.

CAMPHOR

Ellen was becoming more concerned about Dandelion and the way her mind wandered. She always slowed her speech when she spoke and made eye contact with Dandelion to be sure she was listening, but now she wondered if there wasn't something she was unaware of going on with the child. For three days in a row now it seemed to her Dandelion's mind had left her body for no reason at all. And it was scary to Mama Ellen. Yes, she was used to Dandelion being slow in the head and that she understood, but this was different.

Mama Ellen finished cutting the block of camphor gum into a quart jar of Burl's likker. "We'll put the lid on and let it set for a week or so and we'll have good stout camphor to cure our aches," she said looking directly at Dandelion.

Dandelion watched the white pieces float around in the jar. She liked the hazy way it looked before it settled to the bottom. It was the same as it appeared when the humidity was high and it was going to rain. Mama Ellen told the weather by her rheumatism. She rubbed her gnarled hands and said it is going to rain and when Dandelion glanced at the camphor jar on the mantle board, it was cloudy and it always rained, except for winter when it sleeted or snowed.

The strong scent of the camphor settled in Dandelion's throat. It reminded her of last summer when Mama Ellen took her to see Zettie Stillwell's dead baby. The front room windows were closed tight. The baby lay in a small, white box with netting draped over it to keep the flies off its face.

Via Gwynn lived across the hollow from the Stillwells and she was there tending to Zettie. She had already washed the corpse in camphor spirits to keep it from turning black. Dandelion peered in the box at the infant and concluded it wasn't black but rather a faded blue color. The baby was so tiny the copper pennies on each eyelid completely covered the eye sockets. Dandelion stared at the scrawny newborn. Its head was bald like an old man's and the long sleeves of the white cotton gown Aunt Leodia had sewn covered its hands.

As far as Dandelion knew Leodia didn't have any kin in the mountain but everyone referred to her as Aunt. She sewed long white gowns and kept them in her delivery bag. Once she told Mama Ellen that a lot of the mountain people were poor and didn't have anything clean fixed in advance to put on a newborn so she always kept a gown made to bring with her.

Dandelion wondered about the baby's shoes? Its feet were wrapped and the gown tucked under them. She couldn't see any imprint of where the shoes should be. She looked around making sure no one had come back inside and laid her hand in the casket. She touched the feet. All she felt was the wadded material. Quickly working her fingers to loosen the fabric she stuck her hand up the gown. No shoes... cold feet...the smallest hardest feet she had ever felt. The baby reminded Dandelion of her own arm one time when it went numb. She had laid all night with her right arm buckled underneath her and it went to sleep. When she touched it she had no feeling in her skin. That was it exactly. The babies frozen feet had no feeling. She knew why the baby didn't move. Its whole body had gone to sleep.

Dandelion checked the room again and still no one so she lifted the grown and took a quick glance... almost too fast for it to register. No diaper... it was a girl. Dandelion placed the gown as close to how she found it as she remembered and tried to picture in her mind what she saw. The small body had some kind of long tag thing hanging on its little belly. Dandelion's short fingernails were longer than its toes.

The baby's chest rose. Dandelion stood and watched carefully holding her own breath so she could be sure. Dandelion's thoughts were tuned in on the baby so she didn't hear Mama Ellen when she walked up behind her. Mama Ellen touched Dandelion's shoulder and gave her a nudge. "What you thinking?" she asked.

Dandelion didn't speak but she wandered if Mama Ellen knew the baby could breathe. She had always been told when you died the breath left your body.

"Dandelion…you hear me?" Mama Ellen thumped her on the head.

"The baby" she stammered, "It breathed."

"Fool talk," Mama Ellen said, but she stepped close to the casket and moved back the thin curtain so she could get a better view of the baby. A faint rise in its chest sent Mama Ellen screaming for Via.

Via who was busy carrying a bucket of water from the spring thought it was the baby's mother cutting a shine. Then Mama Ellen appeared at the door. "Come, Via, hurry it's the baby. We need Aunt Leodia back to check the baby."

"What on God's good soil?"

"It's the baby…I think it is breathing. Faintly, but good God, I think it is alive!"

Via threw the filled bucket down and rushed into the room. She saw Dandelion standing at the coffin rubbing the baby's hand. She had the wee fingers clasped and was gently patting. The shiny, new pennies were laying to the sides of the baby's head.

Via jerked the infant out of the box and smacked it hard on its back. The baby sucked in its breath and she fell to the floor still clasping the baby.

Later, when things calmed down and the baby's color returned to an ashen pink, Aunt Leodia, rubbing her eyes in disbelief, announced had it not been for Dandelion the unthinkable would of surly happened.

"Dandelion, answer me, girl! Where have you gone off to in that fool head of yours?" Mama Ellen's voice was loud and commanding.

Dandelion opened her eyes and with a shock realized she wasn't at Zettie Stillwell's after all, but instead she lay stretched out at home on Mama Ellen's kitchen floor with a rag soaked in camphor under her noise to revive her.

She shifted her eyes to the table and saw the camphor flakes had settled to the bottom of the likker. They lay an inch thick on the bottom of the jar.

"The flowers of late winter and early spring occupy places in our hearts well out of proportion to their size."

~Gertrude S. Wister

PIG DOLL

Tap, tap, and tap. Three consecutive knocks, knuckles hitting metal, made a thud in the cold December air. Three hops on the left foot and then the right. Dandelion wasn't conscious of her habit but she did everything in threes. Three taps on door knobs before opening, three wishes on a star, even three amen at the end of the Lord's Prayer she had memorized. "Please, please, please, she whispered, her breath cloudy as she bent to feel inside the empty tube.

When she didn't feel anything inside the box she whispered a wishful prayer ending with amen, amen, and amen. Dandelion felt the roaring start in her ears; everyone knew the catalog came the week after Thanksgiving. Lissie and Mullin already had last year's book. They had sneaked it out and hid it in the hollow log at the creek when Tycie's new Sears and Roebook arrived two weeks ago. They had showed it to her, the glossy pages colored with dolls and wicker carriages.

Mama Ellen had told her not to come. "Exposing yourself in this kind of weather will give you pneumonia fever." She had warned. "If the wish book is there, what good is it going to do you? I tell you girl there ain't no such thing as a Santa Claus and Tycie has no business filling those little motherless young'uns heads full of such foolishness…letting them look at the pretties and wish for them knowing there is no chance in hell of them getting anything."

Dandelion couldn't know the pain tainting Mama Ellen. It was something she would never realize. A day was just another happening of events for Dandelion. Although she had the "gift" of seeing, she often didn't understand what she saw. Things happened, people came, and people went passing through the shadows of her mind.

Lissie was satisfied with flipping through the pages of the old catalog. Next fall she would have money of her very own to order whatever she wanted for herself. She especially liked the store bought dresses section. Tycie had told Lissie one of the church women was going to give her a baby pig from the spring litter if she walked her daughter, Hattie, who was in the first grade, to Oak Grove School every morning and made sure she hung her coat and mittens next to the heater to dry before coming back home with her in the afternoons. Lissie was so excited because Tycie had told her if she did this she could raise the shoat and sell it in the late fall. Lissie was sure Tycie would let her keep the money even though she had not said as much.

Dandelion stepped on the foot log and looked at her reflection in the icy creek. She jabbed her balancing stick through the thin crust, one, two, three she said bringing the stick up and down in a churning motion. Instead of her own face she saw the dimpled cheeks of the wish book doll. She could easily find her in the catalog by the bent corner of the page she lived on.

Maybe if it don't come tomorrow Mama Ellen will take me to Tycie's and I can see her new book, Dandelion thought. She hurried along the snow covered path. One, two, and three she counted as she picked the walking stick up and set it back down.

"No!" Mama Ellen said outright, "I ain't a-aiding or a-betting this tom-foolery. You got no business down there, looking at a catalog…a wish book! They would be better off if they hadn't ever seen one their selves. I tell you girl with the shine you are a cutting…running out in the cold every day to check the mail, it is a wander to me you ain't done dead. I have you know we ain't going a knocking on nobody's door to borrow trouble. We got enough already!"

A week before Christmas Lissie came hurrying up through the cow pasture clutching something underneath her coat. Dandelion saw her through the kitchen window and ran out to meet her.

"Look," Lissie squealed. It was the doll from the wish book. Its dimpled checks turned toward Dandelion. The banging noise started in her ears…low at first and got louder and louder until she felt she must scream at Lissie for her to hear. "Where did you get my doll?" Dandelion heard herself say "my" but she didn't mean to.

"Hattie's stupid mama gave it to me." Lissie gulped, tears streaming down her red streaked eyes.

"She bought it for Hattie to give her from Santa Claus but when she seen it she throwed a fit. She had seen another one she loved more so they gave this one to me." Lissie could hardly finish the sentence for the sobs grabbing her throat.

"Why are you crying, crying, crying?" asked Dandelion.

"Because Tycie told me that this was my pig. She said I wouldn't be getting a shoat to raise on my own and sell. She said, "that is your payment for taking care of Hattie, you are holding it in your hands, girl!" Lissie thrust the doll at Dandelion and said, "Here, I don't want this old pig doll, you take it. I never want to see it no more!"

"But, where will I say I got it?" Dandelion asked reaching for the cherished gift.

"Santa Clause, I reckon." Lissie said turning to cross the fence.

"Wait," Dandelion called. Lissie turned to her. "I can't say that because Mama Ellen says they ain't no such thing."

"Well, tell her what you want throw it in the creek for all I care."

Dandelion rushed to her room making sure to stay out of Mama Ellen's sight. She laid the doll on her bed and took its frilly dress off to see if she could put it back on. Then she pulled down its blue bloomers to peek inside. "You are my baby," she said. "I will call you Lovely, you are all mine alone and nobody else's." Dandelion's head pounded and her heart raced. She rubbed the doll's blonde kinky hair and patted it on the head one, two and three. She knew she could never tell Mama Ellen about Santa Claus bringing the doll. She was already mad at him. It would be her secret she decided. Now, where do you keep a secret? Yes, yes, and yes Dandelion rushed out with her doll stuffed in a pillowcase to the hollow log.

Keep your face to the Sunshine
and you will not see the Shadows.

~ Helen Keller ~

Larry Stoneman

FIRE IN THE MOUNTAIN

A sudden fear gripped Dandelion when she felt the March wind start to blow from the north bringing with it thick plumes of smoke.

"Burning brush, I reckon," Mama Ellen said.

Swirls of grey rose higher and fuller and then the chilling sound of church bells echoed through the mountain.

"Wildfire," Ellen hollered, "Lord have mercy with this wind up we are apt to lose everything. Hurry, Dandy, run up on the rock and see if you can tell what all is a burning."

Dandelion stood on the rock looking west. The buzzing started in her ears. She could see the strong wind skipping through the broomstraw field and licking up the sides of Martin's corncrib.

Mama Ellen shook Dandelion by the shoulders snapping her head back and forth, "What is it girl? What did you see?"

"The twins," tears beaded in Dandelion's eyes.

"What?"

"Hurry up with it… how close is the fire?" Mama Ellen capped her apron over her nose to stifle the scorching scent carried by the winds.

Burl came running up the path his face and clothes covered in ash and soot. "It's burning towards the creek. Every man in the country is over there beating it back from Martin's house and barn. If the winds hold from the northwest, it'll likely burn its self out when it gets to the water. We're hunting for those two boys now. Preacher Tom thinks they may have come up this way. Martin thought they were in the house but when they checked they couldn't find them anywhere."

Mama Ellen looked at Dandelion, "You saw them. The twins…"

Dandelion had a blank look in her eyes. "The corn crib", she said staring in the distance, "They went in the crib and the wind blew the door shut making the latch fall."

"Fool talk," Mama Ellen choked.

"Damnation," Burl went lopping back in the direction of the smoke. He ran the distance to the corn crib and unlatched the door.

The twins lay one on top of the other with dried corn shucks covering their heads.

"Here…over here," Burl hollered.

Someone grabbed the boys from his arms. He couldn't see their face in the thick smoke.

Burl heard someone in the yard holler, "take them in the house to their Mammy."

Dandelion held her head in her hands with her thumbs mashing her ears closed to try to shut out the roaring in her head. Smoke blew around the base of the rock but the winds stayed on a steady course. The fire made its way to the creek and was quickly doused by the cold water.

Larry Stoneman

FIFTEEN

Dandelion was fifteen when Mama Ellen caught her rinsing her panties in the little branch. "What nastiness you been up to." She fumed.

Her hateful tone held Dandelion down same as if she had slapped her face. She stared at her feet while hiding the wet panties behind her back. Mama Ellen grabbed Dandelion's arm twisting it around so she could yank the underwear free from her clutch. Holding them up to the sunlight she saw the brown stained crotch. That was when the softness between them was lost. They drifted along not making eye contact when they spoke. And I reckon that is when the biggest hard ball formed in Dandelion's chest. She would feel it growing bigger and bigger until sometimes she couldn't breathe at all. Mama

Ellen said, "Dandelion, when your troubles weigh heavy on you pray and say the calming scriptures like is in Psalms." Then she said, "Yea, though I walk through the shadows of death I will fear no evil: For thou art with me."

Dandelion tried it. When the weather was warm so she could get outside, away from Mama Ellen's prying eyes, it did seem to help with her breathing. It was the winter time that was the worst. They sit around a quilt top, stretched tight in a wooden frame, Mama Ellen next to her watching as she tried to make tiny stitches. She couldn't keep her hands still enough to stay in the chalk tracks drawn across the brightly patterned material. Sometimes the tightness grew in Dandelion until she passed out. Mama Ellen kept the camphor close by to revive her from what she called her "spells."

Dandy learned how to relieve the tightness of that ball. It was simple but brought a lot of misery along with the doing. She thought up cuss words and had ugly thoughts. She closed her eyes tight as she could, squeezed them shut, and let the cuss words she heard Burl say float around in her head. Closed out everything around her and let those words come to her tongue but kept her lips pursed stiff so they couldn't fly out. Mama Ellen sitting there sewing her little stitches with lily white thread knew something was wrong. Sometimes she would say, "Law me, this room is black… it is so dark in here."

You know a body can feel that much hatefulness right there next to them. Late at night if the ball grew to where she couldn't sleep. She whispered those curse words out loud under the cover…

THE MATTOCK

Burl went in and out of the barn sheepishly all morning. Mama Ellen was busy canning cornfield beans and paid no attention to his activity, but Dandelion squatted behind the shrub saw all. She could tell by his walk he was drinking. She couldn't remember her age when she first noticed his high-step and associated it with the smell of alcohol. His meek manner completely changed replaced by a loud, cursing man she hardly recognized as the same person.

Lissie told her Burl planned a frolic for that night. "I heard Daddy and Tycie talking about it," she said. "They are coming and we are coming with them."

Dandelion reckoned that was what all the fuss in the barn was about. He would throw a pitchfork of hay out the main area of the barn and then lean up against the door and wipe sweat. Mama Ellen would be mad if she found out about it. Dandelion thought about telling her just to get Burl put in his place, but she wanted to see Lissie so she kept quiet.

Dandelion squatted behind the boxwood and watched Burl go in and out the barn. He carried boxes and empty feed sacks out to the woodshed. Peeping through the sparse limbs she watched him looking at the house as if he expected something to happen.

Dandelion felt something touch her back. She jerked out of reach and heard Lissie say, "Burl getting ready for the frolic I reckon."

"Where did you come from and how did you see me?"

"Shucks, you ought to know I can smell you. Don't have to use my eyes."

Men with fiddles, banjos and guitars came up the drive followed by women with shoeless children kicking up dust swirls. Mama Ellen came out on the porch to see what was going on.

"Y'all come on up to the house," she invited. They didn't let on they heard her.

Dandelion liked knowing Burl was in trouble bringing this crowd in here. Mama Ellen didn't like drinking and dancing. She saw Mountain Rob sitting on a barrel tuning his banjo. People were still coming, crowding into the barn. Dandelion peeped around a truck and recognized Brody the mountain moonshiner.

She rushed back to the house to tell Mama Ellen what she saw.

"Lord, there will be trouble before this night is done."

"Burl ain't got a bit of gumption when him and the jug get together."

Hoots of laughter and off key singing filled the night air.

"Get in here, Dandelion," Mama Ellen hollered, "and don't waste no time a doing it!"

Dandelion stood by the open window as happy sounds fluttered the lacy curtains. Occasionally someone would holler, "Souy!" She wanted to go outside and play with Lissie, but Mama Ellen wouldn't hear of it. The mantel clock chimed ten times.

Dandelion and Mama Ellen weren't sure if the dance was ending or if the music makers were taking a break. They slipped out to the dark side-porch and listened.

Mullin and Lissie ran into the yard, "A fight!"

"Heaven help us!" Mama Ellen clutched her Bible to her chest.

"A damn killing is the truth of it!" Mullin looked at Ellen.

"Somebody's fixing to get it! Slant-eyed Quinn and Burl are going at each other with mattocks."

"Mattocks?"

"Mullin, what happened?"

"Who knows… just fool drunk I reckon. Slant-eye came down here looking for trouble if you ask me, and, by devil, he has found it. One minute he was sitting out there on the bank smoking and the next thing anybody knew he had a mattock swinging at Burl. You know Burl ain't one to start trouble but he ain't going to run from it either."

Mama Ellen started down the steps when a shotgun fired, "Lord have mercy," she moved faster through the dew covered grass. Dandelion grabbed Lissie's dress to help hold herself up. Quinn lay on his back not moving. Men, women and crying children were running out the road. Little John and Wade helped Quinn's folks load him in the back of their truck. Then they stood back shaking their heads and wiping sweat.

It was a full day before Sheriff Edmonds came for Burl. Mama Ellen hadn't seen him since the night before, but she had a good idea where he was. She opened the door to the cow's stall and there he lay in a devil's dream. He looked like a matted sheep dog the way the clotted blood hung to his head.

Edmonds and two deputies gently pushed Mama Ellen aside and forced Burl to his feet. Dandelion saw the drunken fool had wet his pants.

"Is he all right?"

"Ah, don't worry yourself any over him living. You best be thinking about what is going to happen when those Quinns get done with him. Slant-eye didn't make it. He drew his last breath no sooner than they got him over the mountain. His Pap sent for me well past daybreak."

"He'll make it all right once he sleeps his stupor off."

"Considering the deep hole slant-eye made in his head with the sharp tip mattock, I don't reckon there is anything to take him in over. It is plain to me this is a good case of self-defense! But I aim to lock him up until the corpse is in the ground."

The imaginary smell of dying carnations and death smothered Dandelion pushing her to the ground. It filled her nostrils and lungs, stifling her much like the sight of her dead chick in the jar. Little yellow chick depending on her for food and protection but Burl's foot stilled its breath, it drooped like wilting creasy greens. Dandelion sealed it in a Mason jar and buried the glass container under a pad of moss covered ground. That fall she dug it up, unscrewed the lid, and examined its splintered bones. Tiny skeleton with leg bones no bigger than Mama Ellen's crocheting needles. Darkness settled around Dandelion.

"Have a heart that never hardens, a temper that never tires, a touch that never hurts."

Charles Dickens

Larry Stoneman

PREACHER MIDGET

Burl told Mama Ellen he heard the men at the store talking about they were going to have a preaching midget at Oak Hill Church.

Mama Ellen and Dandelion walked over to the little church. They went early so Mama Ellen could visit with her kin buried in the cemetery. She was pulling crab grass off her daddy's grave when Dandelion peeped around the granite marker and looked straight at that little man. A big tall woman had opened the passenger side door and the preacher hopped out. Dandelion never forgot she was the very first person at the meeting to see him.

The woman had a hinged box full of picture postcards. In the photo the woman sat and the little preacher stood on the piano bench beside her with his hand on her shoulder. He stood at the church door and handed everyone who entered a card.

That tike of a man got up at the pulpit and sang, "Standing on the Solid Rock" before he brought the message. It was the prettiest words Dandelion had ever heard, "Close in our relation, firm in its foundation. I'm standing on the…" She started thinking of Buzzard Rock in connection with the preacher's song. And his booming voice singing about their relation looped around her heart. She rubbed her finger across his face on her card. Ever since, when she climbed the rock she took her image of the midget, and lying flat, she stretched her body out caressing the card in front of her face between her and the heavens. She whispered, "Preacher Midget, when I die let 'em lay me out right here on my rock where I can touch the stars."

Larry Stoneman

BOYFRIEND

On clear summer nights Dandelion liked to climb on her rock and make believe she was a part of the lighted valley world below. Glowing streaks of amber stretched for miles in the distance. If Dandelion had ever been as much as fifty miles to the south of this mountain, she would have recognized Winston Salem to the east, St. Paul to the west, and the village of Ararat to the south of her. Dandelion focused her vision straight out so she wouldn't have to see the lights of Cascade Mountain behind her. They made her

65

angry. So much of this mountain had been bought up by a retired banker and sold off for housing developments.

During the day she couldn't see them but at night their devil lights came on shiny like a fresh cut. It made Dandelion's stomach hurt to look at them: These intruders in search of any rock or ledge to hang a dwelling off of so they could look down on the people in the valley below.

Dandelion was born in this mountain and didn't know anything else so it was different for her to enjoy the night visions. But the banker, who bought out old Man Utt's orchard, had cut it up in lots selling off little plots of mountain soil for these Florida people to spend a few days a year in a cottage was plain destructive as far as she was concerned. They left lights burning when they were gone most of the year.

All Dandelion had to do was catch a glimpse behind her and see an unnatural light high on a post and it made her do things. Like spit in the creek and pee in the road going up to their houses. Most of them put up metal gates to keep people out from places where they had hunted morel mushrooms or ginseng for generations.

She kept her eyes cast down as she climbed the rock so she wouldn't have to see the beams shinning from Cascade and Fox Trot. Tonight she had an imaginary boyfriend who sat snuggled beside her left arm. She talked out loud to him pointing to different colored lights in the distance and pretending she had been to all the places. She had difficulty putting a face on him because she couldn't settle in her mind who she wanted him to be. Leck Gentry's boy

Joseph was by far the best looking one she knew, but he was married to Lula Belle and they had four boys together. After some thought on the matter, Dandelion decided it didn't matter if he was married because nobody would ever find out about him being up here in the dark, just her and him alone in her private place.

"Pluck not the wayside flower;
It is the traveler's dower."

~William Allingham

JOURNEY

Dandelion heard the gravel crunching beneath car tires. She picked up the bag containing her belongings and climbed the familiar route down the rock. She slowly walked the trail past the blackberry vines and woods ferns toward the bend in the road where the social service lady set in her car and waited. Ms. Huntley opened the door of the Dodge with the county plates and watched patiently as Dandelion picked up a handful of dirt and put it in her dress pocket.

"Morning, Dandelion."

Dandelion got in the front seat hugging her paper sack tight against her body. She kept her head down.

"Dozers are busy making way for the new highway," Ms. Huntley said, glancing at Dandelion.

She hadn't figured out what to make of Dandelion. Her body wasn't fully matured like a grown-up's but her face drooped in zigzagged wrinkles giving it the appearance of someone very old.

"Dan-de-lion," the sound of the name rolled around in the car. "I like your name. It reminds me of a yellow flower."

A puff weed, Dandelion thought. Nothing in the world but a bothersome weed that people all around this mountain despises and tries to get rid of as fast as they can.

"We will stop at the Tasty Freeze and get you some ice cream. What do you think, Dandelion? You want a cone of vanilla or chocolate?"

Dandelion didn't answer. She kept her head bent and glanced out the window. She saw a black hen in the ditch just outside the city limits pecking at a worm. Dandelion thought of the time Mama Ellen had the shingles and nothing she tried helped her one bit.

Old Tycie walked up the mountain and stopped by to see them. When she saw how Mama Ellen was suffering. She said, "I can cure you. You wait right here." In a little while she came up the path carrying a black hen by the feet with one hand and her other hand choking it around the neck. Tycie threw the chicken's head across the chopping block and gave a sharp whack with the ax. The old hen's peaked head landed at Dandelion's feet and she looked down in time to see a milky film come up over its eyes as they bore into her.

Tycie held the bleeding hen over Mama Ellen's back and let the warm blood run freely across the blisters. "That's the only thing," Tycie declared, "that'll cure the shingles. The fresh blood of a black hen."

Dandelion stuck her hand in her pocket and cupped up the dry loam. She let it drift through her spread fingers onto the carpeted floor. Ms. Huntley caught the movement and cast her eyes over Dandelion's skinny legs and her dirt-covered shoes, hooked together on the top with big, shiny safety pens. Disbelief shot through Dandelion's body when she felt wetness seep through her clothes and onto the hard, plastic of the seat. First she felt chilled and then hot. Her head dropped lower until her chin rested against the hardness of her breastbone.

When Ms. Huntley stopped the car and shut the driver door, Dandelion managed to roll her eyes to see pictures of ice cream and cola drinks on a board over the top of the restaurant window. Ms. Huntley returned and handed her a cone of soft ice cream. Dandelion couldn't reach for it. She set frozen while the lady placed it in her hand and wrapped her sweaty fingers around the thin, tan cone. Dandelion was stunned as the sticky, sugarberry mixture melted and dripped over her hand and slid into her lap. A throb pounded in and out at her temples and slowly crept down her body. When she was sure Ms. Huntley wasn't looking she willed her hand to move and release the soggy ice cream cone. It left a frothy line along her leg. Picking up her right foot and setting it down on top of the cone took less effort. She squashed it into the black soil on the floor mat.

She heard Mama Ellen saying, "Dandelion, just because you are different don't mean you ain't right in the head."

Working the top of her sack so it wouldn't make a crumpling noise she slipped her hand in the narrow opening and retrieved the tattered card. Holding the picture in front of her mouth and cupping her small hands around it, her thumb caressed the worn place where his face used to be. Dandelion pressed it against her lips and whispered, "Preacher midget, when I die let 'em lay me out on my rock so I can touch the stars."

Larry Stoneman

HOME OF COMFORT

Swing low....sweet chariot... commie forth... Dandelion closed her eyes and let the baritone lull sink in. Oh law, so sweet and deep it caused goose pimples. Commie forth to carry me home...tears overflowed and dripped from her chin.

73

Home, that faraway place tucked in a cove of the Blue Ridge where she had spent every living day for fifty-two years, and now they had forced her to leave. Like a thief in the night she was hurried along and brought to this place where she smelled and tasted the bitterness of her surroundings including the soured feet of the old men hunched over in their drooling sleep.

What had she done to deserve this beyond out living the people who had taken her in as an infant, even though she wasn't of their own flesh, and furnished her a roof over her head and food to eat? That was all... nothing was left to her as her own. Not even a square of soil on which she might have remained in the shadows of home. Home to her was a place, not the wooden and tin structure. The air she breathed floating through an open window after a sprinkle of rain...that was home.

A light flush washed over her. She fidgeted with a balled handkerchief. The whiteness of this place was unsettling. The walls, dresser top, even the cover was all stark.

Mama Ellen never allowed anything white except for the homemade sheets made from bleached Muslim. She said white showed dirt too easily. Dandelion thought it would feel good to see dirt, a smear of red mud or a smudge of black loam. How she longed for something familiar.

"Put your things down and go with me to the dining hall," the woman sitting on the other bed in the narrow room said slipping her pudgy white feet into feathery scuffs as she reached over and turned off her pink, plastic radio.

Dandelion set her bag on the cot assigned to her and followed the woman.

"My name is Rose," she said.

Rose of Sharon, Dandelion thought not raising her head or speaking. A verse from the Bible she had heard Mama Ellen recite came to her mind, "I am the rose of Sharon, and the lily of the valley." (Solomon 2:1). Mama Ellen gave the book and verse after the scripture. So even though Dandelion couldn't read she had many verses memorized. It calmed her to whisper them to herself when she was upset. And this usually happened when she was around people, especially strangers. She held her wadded handkerchief up over her mouth and made little whistling noises with her teeth and tongue as the words came out. Dandelion didn't realize this was one of the things people found odd about her. They couldn't hear what she was saying. They just saw a small hunched over figure mumbling into a cotton handkerchief.

Dandelion followed Rose into the crowded dining room. The food smelled good. A tall metal cart on wheels stood in the middle of the floor. It held rows of trays with people's names printed on cards telling who got which plate. Dandelion sat next to Rose. She felt humiliation swell in her as a woman wearing a checked smock tied a terry cloth bib around her neck. Dandelion put her hand over her mouth and in a voice barely audible recited John 3:16. "For God so loved the world...."

"What?" Rose looked at her.

Dandelion didn't notice the interruption. She ate the bland food and drank the bitter tea not knowing the small paper packets contained salt, pepper, and sugar.

After the meal Rose led Dandelion outside to sit on a long, rocker filled porch. In the distance was many smoke stacks shooting puffs of white steam and embers towards the sky.

A fat, grey cat lay beside Dandelion's chair. Once they had a tomcat that peed on her bed and the odor wouldn't wash out of her quilt. Seemed to Dandelion she could always smell that cat pee.

The small plot of grass they called the lawn was enclosed by a tall iron fence keeping people inside but the view of rusty cars and rotting sheds next door were clear. Dandelion felt trapped and afraid.

"Jesus wept. John 3:16."

"What did you say?"

Dandelion didn't answer but she did notice Rose's foot quit swinging as she set forward planting both feet firmly on the floor.

"Why did they send you here anyway? What is the matter with you? You don't walk in your sleep do you? You go around with your eyes half shut like Emma, my last roommate? She plundered my stuff during the night. They said she was walking in her sleep and didn't remember anything about it after she woke up, but I didn't fall for that tale. I told them that's her tale and I sit on mine."

"Now don't be messing in my belongings. I'll tell you right now, I am easy enough to get along with but I don't aim to put up with no stealing!"

Dandelion knew Rose was mad by the tone of her voice. She thought about the meaning of what Rose had said. She wasn't sure, but it did look to her like Rose had a lot of stuff. She covered her mouth, "Thou shalt not steal, Exodus 20:15."

"What, what did you say? Are you some kind of mute or crazy or what?"

Rose was sorry as soon as the question came out. Thinking it would please Dandelion, she tried to put the big, furry tom on her lap.

"Here, hold it, he won't scratch. They've had its claws pulled out."

It wasn't its claws that bothered Dandelion. She flat didn't want to hold no stinking cat so she curved her body inward folding over until her head rested on her knees.

Rose dropped the cat on the floor and went inside without a backward glance.

Dandelion's heart raced. She didn't know how to get back to their room. She followed quickly trying to keep Rose's moving feet in view but she lost sight of her and meandered along slowly peeping in every door. She scanned the floors for Rose's furry slippers.

Then she heard it. The sweet, soft floating music and knew. That was it... the room with Rose and her radio and her music and her stuff. Yes, Dandelion thought as she entered the white room and saw her paper bag setting undisturbed on the bed. She covered her mouth and whispered, "Let the day perish wherein I was born, Job 3:3."

She says to Rose a Sharon, quiet as a whisper, "Damn you, for having all that stuff and never knowing the fear of a long night. You lay there in a pink cloud with your feathered blindfold covering squinted eyes and snort like an old sow hog."

Shadows from the yard light create dancing ghosts on the ceiling. Most times Dandelion gets up and sits in her straight chair and stares at the bright hall so they will go away.

"Hell," she says right out loud "what a damnation of a place!" She hears somebody hollering. The muffled noise sounds like it is coming through a tunnel. The only way to shut the sound out is by holding her breath and thinking black thoughts. She feels light-headed like she is going to pass out until she sucks in a big mouthful of air. She thinks any time now she will decide not to breathe. Then she could float out of this place. Rise up like the hot air balloon Burl told her about seeing in France during the war. In the wee hours just before day, the mugginess grows thick with the stench of piss and people's filth. It presses hard as a cannon ball against her spiny breast bone. She pulls her white bedcover under her chin. Her small body trembles the sheets which feel as cold as the icy metal bed frame. "Owl shit," she whispers over and over until the grip of that knot eases so she can doze.

THE LETTER

Dandelion raked at a piece of crispy bacon with her fork. Finally it fell off the side of her plate. "Burnt plumb black is what that is," she mumbled into her cloth napkin.

Although Rose's elbow was against Dandelion's arm she didn't bother to glance up. The only time Dandelion spoke to anyone was when she complained. If she wasn't sick, then it was too hot to go outside, or she was afraid she would get a smudge on her white sheets.

Rose was a free spirit and wasn't used to being around a pessimist like Dandelion. She found the best way for her to get along with her roommate was to ignore her and this seemed to suit Dandelion. They had unconsciously formed a habit of being together without socializing. Dandelion lacked the skills and Rose was short on patience.

Rose went to sit in the solarium after eating and Dandelion followed, head bent, in her footsteps. They didn't return to their room until almost noon.

Rose saw the envelope propped against her table lamp. She had to look at it twice before she was sure she was seeing right.

"Here, you got a letter!"

"Ain't no letter of mine! Quit your fooling! My head hurts!"

"Look," Rose shoved the sealed envelope at Dandelion.

"Whose it from?" Dandelion saw the loopy letters running across the pink envelope and the perfectly shaped lilac bloom, its purple head barely peeping out from under the sealed flap.

"Here Rose, see who it is from and what they want."

"Well, it sure smells flowery. My guess is it is from someone fancy." Rose ran her metal nail file under the fold and cut it see-saw like until she retrieved the stationary.

"I have never had a real letter before; Rose, read the name so I will know who is doing the talking."

Dandelion held her breath and craned her head to the side to quiet the swooshing noise in her ears. She learned years earlier what she had to do when this roar started bringing flickers of lights in front of her eyes. Rose turned the single sheet of paper over and read the signature on the back, "Lissie."

"I am not reading a word more til you tell me about this Lissie person? There ain't a soul one been here to visit since the day you stumbled into my room. It is just like you was a newborn calf with nobody to do the licking off. You just sit around humped-up looking off in the distance or staring at people's feet til they think you are some kind of mute."

"What's this?" Rose opened a small piece of folded yellowed paper. A dried leaf fell onto Dandelion's bed.

"A four leaf clover," Dandelion sighed. And the smell of home was perfumed with mountain lilacs and fresh cut field grass.

"Look at this old tarnished paper. It is covered with X's and O's."

Dandelion took the aged paper and silently read the penciled letters as hugs and kisses. The X's started at the top corner and zigzagged down the middle ending in O.

"Ok, tell all…who is this Lissie person?"

Dandelion dropped her head and twisted a strand of her thin fine hair between shaky fingers. She wanted to tell Rose about Lissie and Mullin, but she couldn't form the words. How does one say what they feel when it makes the heart ache? She saw Lissie plain, sitting on their favorite log by the spring. Heard her explaining what it meant to turn from a girl into a woman. She didn't have to hide what she felt from Mullin and Lissie.

Dandelion wandered what Rose would say if she knew that as a baby she was pulled out of a rusty stove pipe in the orchard where her own blood mother had thrown her away. Rose with her fluffy pink things and dusting powder would never understand.

"Just a neighbor girl that grew up below me," Dandelion said, "now quit this chatter and read me my letter, Rose."

"All right."

"'Dear Dandelion,'"
I have worked for a month to find your address. The other day I went down to Sinus' store and that woman from the county was there snooping around asking ole man Sinus questions about different families around here. I butted in and told her I needed to know where I could write to you and she printed this address down for me. I sure hope this reaches you and finds you well.

I am enclosing a paper I found in Mullin's things. He had written your name on it and I felt it only right you get it. He would have wanted it that way. He didn't leave much behind. He went easy like. Little Litt found him folded over on the side of the road going into Shad Cove. He went for the doctor but there weren't nothing could be done.

We the only two left over here now.... I am still talking like you are here. I keep praying you will get to come back to the mountain, but I reckon I am talking to the air. They done put your marker up out at the church. That's where Mullin found the four leaf clover. He showed it to me the day he found it. 'Look, Liss, what I found on Dandy's grave.' That's what he called it. When you left home it was same as if you were dead to him. I reckon he knew better than me that you'd not be coming back. After them strangers took over Mama Ellen's place, they had your tombstone put up even cut your name and birth date into it. Nothing left to do but dig six foot and cut the date of death. Well, I needn't talk. My name is cut on the stone beside of Mullin's. I didn't see the sense in putting up two stones when one would do just fine. The man said he wouldn't charge nothing extra to cut mine while he was here. There is one thing I want you to know and never doubt it for one minute and that is Mullin loved you. I know he was backward like and wouldn't let on but there are some things a sister can tell.

I should have told you long before now, so you could have had the peace in knowing you were loved.

It is so lonely here with only the sounds of the whippoorwills hollering to answer me. The new road brings in a few travelers. They shop with Sinus' people at the store. Buy pop and picnic supplies.

"'Lissie'"

Dandelion placed the fragile clover leaf back in the tainted paper. She folded it like it had been, being careful to follow the creased lines. Each "X" and "O" perfectly folded as Mullin had done with his own hands only God knew when. She held it up to her face making sure to block Rose's view. She kissed it, just a quick peck, and put it in her treasured paper sack of stuff.

First you see me in the grass dressed in yellow gay; next I am in dainty white, then I fly away.

THE DAY THAT DIDN'T DAWN

Rose opened her eyes. Sitting up in bed and looking around the room she saw light from the hallway filtering underneath her door. She noticed the bedside clock said seven o'clock. Was it morning?

Outside the window hung a cloudy mist of fog shrouding the lamppost, reflecting a pinkish glow on the world.

Startled awake by a sound in the hallway? That was it or was it?

The room didn't feel right. Dandelion's chair by the window was empty. She was always hunched in her chair by daybreak every morning.

Rose felt sick, a kind of blank empty feeling like a hunger deep inside similar to static air before thunder announces a summer storm.

The vastness of her surroundings added to the discomfort. She was waiting for something but wasn't sure what. Dandelion's cot was empty. Her things cleared from the room.

"Preacher Midget, when I die let 'em lay me on my rock
so I can touch the stars."

Special thanks to my talented friends for helping make the publication of Dandelion's story possible: Shelby Inscore Puckett, who gave unselfishly of her time and knowledge.
Wayne Easter, Nancy Johnson, Kimberly Burnette-Dean and Larry Stoneman for generously sharing their art of photography.
Thanks with love to Elke for her support.